iUniverse books may be ordered through booksellers or by contacting:

iUniverse
1663 Liberty Drive
Bloomington, IN 47403
www.iuniverse.com
844-349-9409

Because of the dynamic nature of the Internet, any web addresses or links contained in this book may have changed since publication and may no longer be valid. The views expressed in this work are solely those of the author and do not necessarily reflect the views of the publisher, and the publisher hereby disclaims any responsibility for them.

Any people depicted in stock imagery provided by Getty Images are models, and such images are being used for illustrative purposes only.
Certain stock imagery © Getty Images.

ISBN: 978-1-6632-5477-1 (sc)
ISBN: 978-1-6632-5475-7 (hc)
ISBN: 978-1-6632-5476-4 (e)

Library of Congress Control Number: 2024902103

Print information available on the last page.

iUniverse rev. date: 08/22/2024

THUNDERSTORM COMES TO TEXAS

Book Three of the Adventures Dogs Series

Written by

KATHY PRIEST-SMITH

This is my third book in the adventures Dogs series. i dedicate this special book to my two daughters, alyssa and Morgen. you both have made me proud even though we have our ups and downs. Thank you for believing in my books and encouraging my writing. i love you both. While you were both growing up, and i read to you, i never dreamed i would write a book, which you both would read.

German shorthaired pointers became a new breed of dog in the 1800s and were thought to come out of Germany. They were born out of combining many different Pointer dog breeds until they became the German shorthaired pointer-a perfect hunting dog for land and water. This breed gained recognition by the American Kennel Club in the 1930s. The German shorthaired pointer (GSP for short) is a highly active dog, whose weight and diet must be monitored, just like we do our Great Dane, Millie.

These dogs are highly intelligent and great with children. The drawback is they do need lots of attention and interaction as they will have the tendency to get into mischief. Their mischief can include, but is not limited to, tearing up their toys and beds, and tearing up shoes, mail, and packages. Any high energy dog will exhibit this type of behavior. Since they are a very energetic breed, a large number of rescue centers for the German shorthaired pointers have been established all over the United States. Please make sure you do your homework and are able to spend the required time with this breed. Maybe even consider adopting or rescuing an adult German shorthaired pointer instead of getting a young puppy.

I hope you all will enjoy reading this book, especially for those who read the second book and are waiting for answers to the mysterious ending to Annie's book.

This is the link to the rescue center in Texas for German shorthaired pointers that are in the rescue facility:

texasgsprescue.com

Annie is a female German shorthaired pointer and I, Millie, am a female Great Dane and currently we get left alone a lot these days. Our owners Kathy and Greg, are busy with work, but on weekends we usually have more family time with them. Sometimes Kathy is gone, and sometimes Greg is gone, and sometimes they both are gone. I miss them so much when they are both gone!

Annie has become more playful our first year together in our forever home, but she stays in her kennel when it rains. It doesn't rain very often in Texas, and Annie is afraid of rain. I have no one to play with when it rains. The backyard where our humans planted grass still has not grown, so there is lots of mud and we track it inside. Annie needs to get over her fear of rain, and only she knows why it frightens her since it rarely rains.

It is the weekend and both of our owners have left this time. I think something is going on because they took Landon and Peyton, the grandchildren, with them and lots of suitcases. Annie says it is nothing. I think they are getting Annie and me a surprise. Guess what? Annie is wrong. There is something big going to happen, and both of our lives will change! Before we know it, here comes Peyton, Landon, Greg, and Kathy with a yapping surprise.

My name is Mountain Thunderstorm, but I am known as Storm or Stormy. I was born in Oklahoma. My current owners have a nice home and two loving children. Their dad, Mark, purchased me to be a bird dog hunter and an inside pet for his children. I grew up playing with a ball in my mouth. I did great in hunting school, but when not on point, I wanted to always play ball. Some humans may say I am obsessed with my red, spiny plastic ball.

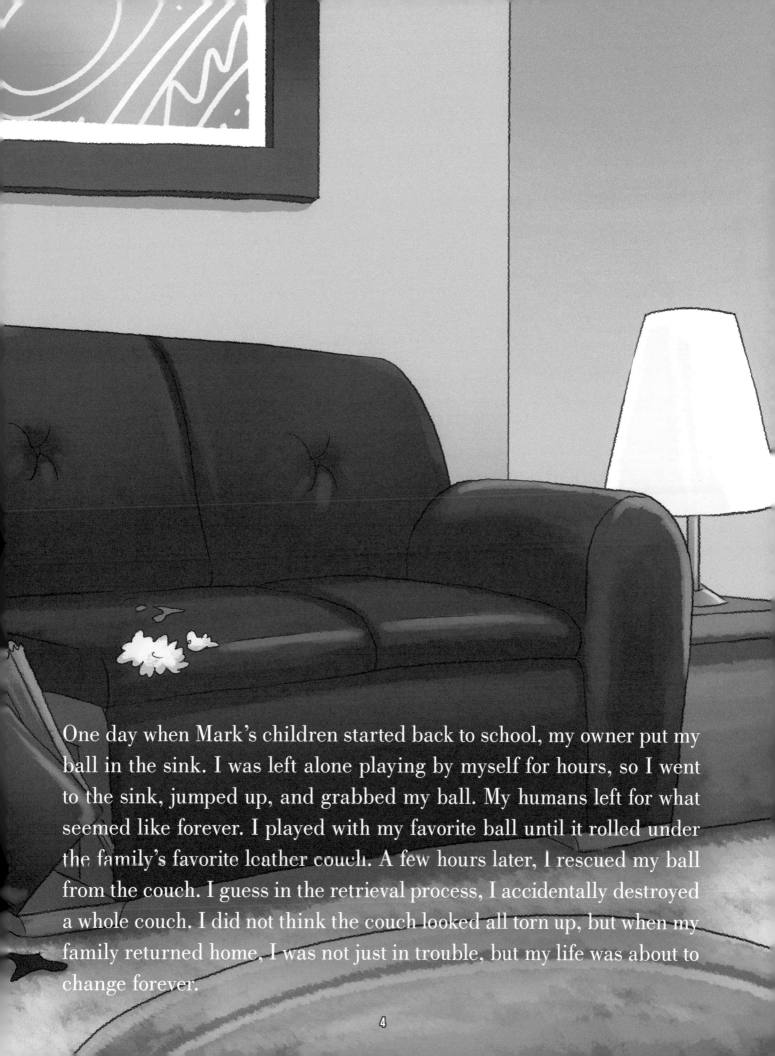

One day when Mark's children started back to school, my owner put my ball in the sink. I was left alone playing by myself for hours, so I went to the sink, jumped up, and grabbed my ball. My humans left for what seemed like forever. I played with my favorite ball until it rolled under the family's favorite leather couch. A few hours later, I rescued my ball from the couch. I guess in the retrieval process, I accidentally destroyed a whole couch. I did not think the couch looked all torn up, but when my family returned home, I was not just in trouble, but my life was about to change forever.

I have grown a lot since I was a pup. I am an adorable black and white ticked and spotted male German shorthaired pointer. I'm about one year old. A month or so later after the "couch incident," Mark's parents put me and all my belongings into their vehicle and we drove and drove. They took me to a parking lot in Fort Worth, Texas.

Next to their vehicle was a big black truck with two adults and two children. All four got out of the truck and introduced themselves to Mark's parents. The adult female named Kathy took my leash and walked me around while petting me. The male that was with her named Greg put all my belongings into the back of the black truck. The two children "rock-paper-scissored" to see who sat next to me.

Eventually, I sat in the back between, Peyton and Landon. They petted and rubbed me the whole way to San Angelo, Texas. Everyone in the truck wanted me to be calm and not scared. Scared-no--confused-yes! The big black truck pulled into a driveway of a house, and Greg took me into the backyard. Kathy, Peyton and Landon went into the house.

A few minutes later, I see Greg open the back door, and a female dog that looks like me runs out of the house. Her name is Annie, and she is a GSP like me, but she is liver colored, a dark reddish-brown with white spots and ticking. I found out later that I am their surprise.

We chase each other all over the yard. I am very fast and athletic. A few minutes later, another dog comes out of the house. This time it is a tall black dog. She is very tall. Her name is Millie and she is a Great Dane. The three of us run, jump, and play together. We sniff noses and behinds. I let Annie and Millie know that I am Storm and from very far away.

I left out the part about the couch and the leaving my home. I wanted them to like me since I think I am not going back to Oklahoma. Millie and I have something in common because we were both rescued. She had to leave her home, and I definitely left my home. She is strong and loves to play with toys just as much as I do. I am so happy that I have two friends to play with in this new home.

My old family did send with me the red "couch" ball and my white soccer ball. Millie must be smart to catch me in the backyard. I am so excited! She likes to play soccer, especially when Greg plays with us. He kicks the ball and then the two of us go after it. I get the ball and then Millie's mouth takes it away from me. If she does drop it, then I nose it up in the air. I can jump over Millie or go under her. What fun!

Annie does not play soccer, but she does like to play chase and hide-n-seek.

I have a lot of fun running all over the yard. I really love my red rubber spiked ball. I play catch and fetch with Greg. When Annie steals my rubber ball, she tries to eat it! I must keep my toy ball away from Annie or she will eat it and nothing will be left. Millie loves to chew on my toys while getting slobber all over them-yuck! Her slobber sure does make my toys slippery and gooey.

I came to my new home in Texas during October. It was a lot hotter than Oklahoma, but now that it is November, it is starting to get cooler. One of the humans, Daylan, Greg's son, takes all 3 of us to the dog park. A dog park is a big fenced in area with some grass and trees and most of the time there's lots of dogs. We all love going to this park. The three of us have made many dog friends. Millie has actually met another Great Dane in the park. Annie and I have met many German shorthaired pointers.

In late November, Annie stopped going to the dog park. She cannot go to the dog park since there are so many other dogs that might bother her since she's not herself. Annie gets upset being left alone, and I feel bad she cannot go. Annie is giving off a scent that makes other male dogs want to be close to her and bother her. Annie must stay home to be safe because if she growls at a male dog at the dog park, she might get hurt! I love the scent she gives off because it does make me go a little crazy. I want to be near her and snuggle her, but right now she growls when I get close.

Finally, Annie allows me to be near her again. The ten days of her ignoring Millie and me were awful. Even Millie was upset with me because all I wanted to do was play with Annie. Ten days later, all three of us are back playing together. Annie did seem a little different now. Instead of playing chase, she wants to play with just me. Annie nudges me with her nose and then jumps up and bows down, and then I do the same to her. Millie feels left out now, but I have to admit, when I play with Annie I do not even think about my red ball.

November went by fast and now it is December and really cold. Annie has started gaining weight. I am about to go to a hunting camp for four weeks. I will miss Annie and Millie, but I love to hunt more than I love to play ball.

My hunting camp is in Christoval, Texas. David, who works with me at his house on ranch property, has lots of different birds. I am learning to find the birds in difficult areas of the ranch. I point, flush out, and retrieve them. When David is ready, I flush the birds out of hiding and into the air so David can shoot at the birds. If a bird falls to the ground, I go and retrieve the bird. If it is near me, I just point at the bird. At first, I am on a long tether, which is like a leash but lots longer. After a few weeks, I am released without any tether to show what David has taught me. David praises me all the time, so I must be good at hunting. I do not even miss my family or my red ball. I hope that I hid my red ball well enough so they do not get it while I am gone.

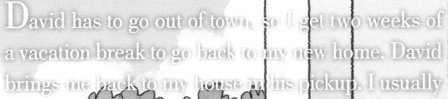

David has to go out of town, so I get two weeks of a vacation break to go back to my new home. David brings me back to my house in his pickup. I usually ride in the back of his vehicle when we hunt, but today he lets me sit up front. When we get to the house, Greg meets us outside. David tells Greg I am doing great. I will be going back in two weeks to finish my training. He also sends Greg some videos of me hunting

I am so anxious to see my pack mates, Annie and Millie. They meet me at the door. Oh, my goodness. Annie is a lot bigger than I remember. Millie slobbers all over me and has not changed a bit. Millie is ready to play. I start looking for where I left my red ball.

The toys, including my red ball, I find are now outside in a wooden locker. Greg gets my red ball and we start playing catch. While we are playing ball, Annie lies in the sun outside. Millie tries to get the red ball, but I am faster than she is. I could play ball all day.

December is almost over now. I am not sure what Christmas is, but there is a tree in the corner of the living room with a fence around it. On this day, we have lots of wrapped toys under the tree and in stockings. After all the packages are opened, there is paper, boxes, ribbons, and tags all over the living room where our kennels sit. Kathy and Greg let us play outside with all the new toys. Annie, Millie and I spent most of our time pulling on the same toy. You would think with all these toys, we would each pick a different one. No! We all want the same toy, which is the long rope with bones tied on each end.

We also got a special meal on this day. Greg puts some turkey meat on our food and mixes it up. It was so good, we all finished about the same time. Millie usually is the first one through and Annie is the last, but today it was a three-way tie. We all agree that we like this day of Christmas.

It is the first week of January and a new year. I will be going back to hunting camp in a few days. Annie is sleeping a lot, and she is not eating much. I hope she is not sick. Well, she must be sick, she threw up...gross! Greg lets her lay down beside him on the couch for the night. It is almost midnight and Annie is moaning and making awful howling sounds. Greg has moved her to her kennel. He is sitting on the floor by her side with her head in his lap. Kathy put Millie and I outside with my red ball.

Kathy keeps on going from the kennel where Annie is laying and back to check on us outside. The time seems to go by slowly when you are outside in the dark on a cloudy night, while it's a little cool. Millie and I get bored playing ball. We are both staring through the back door glass panels. Millie and I do not know what is happening! We turn to look at each other with hopes that Annie will be OK!

The End

...to be continued in our next book between Christmas 2024 and Easter 2025.

Game Instructions:

Storm loves his spiny, red rubber ball. Please help Storm find his
ball. His ball may be lost on the page or in his mouth. They are
all over this book. Please see how many you can find.